Copyright © 1985 Award Publications Limited

First published in USA 1985
by Exeter Books
Distributed by Bookthrift
Exeter is a trademark of Simon & Schuster, Inc.
Bookthrift is a registered trademark of Simon & Schuster, Inc.
New York, New York

ISBN 0-671-07515-2

Printed in Belgium

MY BEDTIME
stories

Written by Hayden McAllister

NEW YORK

Raymond the Flying Rabbit

The crowd cheered as the circus master announced:
"Ladies and gentlemen; we present, Raymond the Flying
Rabbit!"

Porky Pig rolled out the cannon with Raymond already
packed inside. Everyone held their breath while Willie Mouse
lit the fuse. There was a sizzle, a crackle and then a *great* big
BANG!

The next moment Raymond the Flying Rabbit was flying
through the air! (Inside his colored waistcoat he wore his
special rabbit parachute).

One day Raymond hopes to be the first rabbit on the moon.

Bubbles

Benny Bear had a bubble pipe.

Benny liked to sit in his deck chair and blow bubbles into the sky.

One day a little mouse called Millie came to watch Benny blowing bubbles. Millie enjoyed watching the bubbles floating into the air. So Benny gave her a tiny bubble pipe as a present.

Later, Millie brought her own little deck chair and placed it beside Benny's big deck chair. Then they *both* blew bubbles in the sunshine.

Feeding the Ducks

Sam Bear and his mother liked to go and feed the ducks in the park. Mama would save some scraps of bread and put them in a special bag marked DUCKS.

After shopping, Sam and his mama would take the bag of duck food down off the shelf and go out to the pond in the park.

One of the ducks had some little chicks and Sam and his mother liked to be sure that the chicks had plenty of bread to eat so they would grow big and strong.

The Echo

Colin the Cat was strolling down the street with his guitar on his back. "Tra la la," he sang. "Tra la lo."

Suddenly Colin the Cat heard an echo! "Tra la la," it went. "Tra la lo!" "I like it," purred Colin. "I like it! If only I could take the echo around with me."

A moment later a little Canary fluttered down onto the top of Colin's guitar, and sang: "Tra la la. Tra la lo!"

Bonzo's Ball

Bonzo liked to chase the rabbits across Bunny Meadow. It was his favorite game. But the rabbits of Bunny Meadow soon grew fed up with Bonzo. They liked to nibble the grass in peace, and they didn't like Bonzo chasing them.

One day the chief rabbit had an idea. He gave Bonzo a colored ball to play with. Bonzo was very pleased!

Now Bonzo chases the rubber ball instead of the rabbits of Bunny Meadow.

Magic Carpet Music

Tom and Sally along with Benji their dog were sitting on the fireside carpet while their mother was making the dinner.

Tom was learning to play his trumpet. Sally was reading a story about a magic carpet, and Benji was yawning.

Suddenly Tom said: "Listen to this tune called 'Dream Time'". As Tom began to play his trumpet they all seemed to be floating away. Sally couldn't believe her eyes! She could see their house below and the green hills far away. She was wondering how they were going to get back home when Tom said: "Wake up Sally. Dinner is ready."

Monkey Bridge

The three monkeys were standing on the banks of the river. The river was very deep. And the current was very strong.

"We'd better cross at the wooden bridge," said the first monkey.

"Yes. It will be much safer than trying to swim across," agreed the second monkey.

"I can't swim anyway," admitted the third monkey.

When the three monkeys reached the bridge they found it had been swept away by the river.

Luckily for them, a friendly crocodile called Eustace was passing by and he offered to help.

"I'll lie across the river, and you can all walk across me as if I were a log," suggested Eustace.

The first monkey walked across Eustace safely. But the third monkey was so frightened that the second monkey had to give him a piggy-back across.

"Thank you very much," chorused the three monkeys when they reached the far bank.

"Have a nice day," said the crocodile.

The Six Rabbits

There were six rabbits who lived in a warren in the middle of a big meadow. They were all different sizes. One was tall, and he had a high voice.

Another was small and round and he had a deep, low voice.

All six rabbits could sing beautifully, and one day it occurred to them to form a choir.

Every Saturday afternoon the six rabbits would give a choir concert in the middle of the wood.

Birds and mice and sometimes a hedgehog would come to hear them sing.

The six rabbits wrote their own words and music and they sang about trees and stars and birds and mice and hedgehogs…and rabbits!

Baking a Cake

Mother Bear was baking.

She had made some little honey cakes for tea, and now she was making bread. Laura Bear wanted to make a cake too. So her mama gave her a piece of dough. Laura roled the piece of dough until it was flat. Then she moulded it into a teddy bear shape.

"I'll put it in the oven with the bread," said Mrs Bear. "When it has been baked it should turn golden brown."

"Oh good!" said Laura, "then it will be just *like* a teddy bear!" When Father Bear came home, Laura gave the pastry teddy bear to him.

"It's just what I've always wanted," said Father Bear with a smile.

Ralph Rabbit

Ralph Rabbit had a home-made wheelbarrow.

He had made it himself, fixing two wheels and two handles to an old wooden box.

Ralph liked to wander along country paths pushing his wheelbarrow.

Sometimes he would walk for miles.

Ralph had a friend called Delia Duck. Delia was a big white farmyard duck and she didn't like walking *too* far.

So when Delia saw Ralph out walking she would hitch a ride in his wheelbarrow!

Acorn Sums

Bob the Squirrel had made his home inside an oak tree.

During the autumn he had collected and stored away plenty of acorns to keep himself alive through the cold winter months.

Bob was a very clever squirrel, for while other squirrels slept during the winter months, Bob was learning sums!

To teach himself to count, Bob made himself a little counting frame out of acorns and twigs.

Bob was learning very *fast* with his acorn abacus. He knew that as soon as he had learnt *all* his lessons he would be able to eat the acorns!

Sarah

Sarah Rabbit loved to knit.

She could knit scarves, hats, jumpers and woollen boots for any rabbit.

Sarah liked to use wool of many different colors.

She had made a red scarf, a blue hat and a yellow jumper in only one week. Next week she was going to knit a pair of mittens for herself. That was to stop her paws from getting cold in the winter.

With warm paws, Sarah could knit lots of winter gifts for her rabbit friends.

Shipwrecked Fox

Ferdy the Fox was stranded on a tiny desert island. His boat had sunk and the only thing Ferdy had been able to save was his banjo and a big tin of candies.

But Ferdy didn't mind. It was nice to be away from the noise of the big city where he lived.

As he sat there under the single palm tree playing his banjo, the sea made soothing noises as it lapped on the sand. Ferdy reached out and picked up a coconut that had fallen from the palm tree and poured himself a drink of coconut milk.

"This is the life," said Ferdy, dipping into his tin of candies.

"Ugh!" spluttered Ferdy.

"Peppermint! I *hate* peppermint! Why couldn't I be shipwrecked with a tin of chicken flavored candies?!"

Joe and Bluebell

Joe was a rabbit who loved to go walking in the countryside. He walked to the fields every day to collect some juicy grass to eat. Sometimes Joe found a carrot or two.

There was a donkey called Bluebell in one of the fields and if Joe had a spare carrot he would take it along for Bluebell to eat. Bluebell and Joe would talk for hours. They would tell each other exciting stories.

Two or three friendly songbirds would perch on the fence to listen to their tales.

When Joe and Bluebell had finished talking, the birds would sing a 'thank you' song and their bird music would make Joe and Bluebell feel very happy and contented.

Pixie Paula

Paula was a pixie who lived in a pixie house in a peaceful part of the wood

Paula loved music. She could sing beautiful songs with her soft pixie voice all day long, and often entertained her friends who lived in the wood.

One day her grandfather gave her a pixie flute made out of wood of an old plum tree.

Paula tried to play her flute amongst the trees and the woodland flowers. The sound of her playing made the wood mice and other friends come out to see what was happening. It was some time before everyone agreed that Paula's present had been a good idea!

Bingo's Dreams

Bingo the Dog liked to lie in front of the fire. It was his favorite place.

Once Bingo had settled down it didn't take long for him to go to sleep. When he was asleep, Bingo would often dream. Sometimes he would dream he was chasing rabbits across a big wide meadow.

Bingo usually felt very tired after chasing those dream rabbits. So when he awoke he was always pleased to find himself back home, beside a nice warm fire, lying on his favorite rug.

Fox In a Fix

Roger the Rabbit and Rob the Red Squirrel both knew a cosy hollow where they could lie down and snooze in the sunshine. It was full of soft green grass and buttercups. Because it was their favorite place, Roger and Rob had hidden some carrots and acorns there in an oak tree pantry.

When Ferdy the Fox heard about this he hid in a tree and waited for the two friends to come along. But both Roger and Rob had keen eyesight and they saw Ferdy the Fox long before he saw them. So instead of leading Ferdy to their oak tree pantry they led him into the back garden of their friend Joe Bear who chased the fox away with a growl.

Water Skiing

Bob the Bear had been invited to visit his friend Ben for the weekend.

Ben the Bear lived by the ocean, so Bob took his water skis along. On the first afternoon, Ben hired a motor boat and both he and Bob went boating together.

The next afternoon, Bob put on his water skis while Ben tied a length of rope to the back of the motor boat.

Ben started the motor boat and Bob hung on tightly to the rope. In no time at all Bob was whizzing along on his water skis behind the motor boat.

"We'll have to do this more often," beamed Bob.

"Yes! Why not come down again next weekend!" said Ben.

Bronco Bear

Broncho Bear wanted to be a cowboy. For his birthday his mama made him a cowboy hat.

Broncho's pa was a carpenter, and he made Broncho a wooden horse which had four wheels.

Broncho liked to take his horse into the garden and ride it up and down the lawn. He hoped that one day he would meet a *real* cowboy.

When dinner time came, Broncho's mama made him some beans on toast which was a *real* cowboy meal.

The Sad Frog

Mr Dragonfly saw a sad looking frog sitting alone on the side of a pool.

"Cheer up Mr Frog," said the dragonfly as it hummed through the air.

"Cheer up," sighed Mr Frog. "I can't. I wish I could."

"But what is wrong?" asked Mr Dragonfly, circling around the frog's head. "Perhaps I can help?"

"Wrong!" muttered Mr Frog. "The worst thing that could happen to a frog – that's what's wrong…I've lost my *croak*."

"Poor Mr Frog," soothed the dragonfly. "What do you think happened to your croak?"

"I think I must have forgotten *how* to croak," muttered Mr Frog.

"I'm sure you haven't," said Mr Dragonfly. "You just stopped croaking because you're not happy. I'll try and cheer you up."

With that the dragonfly landed on top of the frog's head and began to tickle him.

Soon Mr Frog couldn't stop laughing.

"Croak, croak," he said. "Croak, croak. Please stop tickling my head!"

The Toy Train

Rupert the Rabbit had a toy train. There was a red engine and three yellow trucks which Rupert pulled along with a piece of string.

Every day Rupert the Rabbit had lots of adventures with his toy train. When bedtime came, Rupert used his bed as a tunnel several times before resting his train in the corner of his bedroom.

One day Rupert's pa made a garage for the train out of a cardboard box. So before Rupert went to bed, he could put his toy train to bed first.

Old Bob Rabbit

Old Bob Rabbit was a watchmaker. He had a little shop in Rabbit Village where he could mend clocks and watches.

Bob could fix big clocks, small clocks, wristwatches and pocketwatches. He had once mended the famous church clock in Rabbit Village after it had broken down.

Old Bob loved his work so much that he was not a good timekeeper. His wife, Mrs Mary Rabbit became very cross because he was always late for dinner. So she made him set an alarm clock to tell him when it was time to close the shop and go home.

A Day Off

"Whose idea was it to clean windows for a living?" groaned Chuck Chimp.

"It was *your* idea," replied his pals, Chick and Chip.

"Well my arms are killing me," moaned Chuck Chimp. "Rub, rub. Polish, polish. Up and down those ladders all day."

"But it keeps you fit," chorused Chick and Chip.

"Fit to drop," groaned Chuck Chimp.

"Okay," said Chick to Chuck. "Tomorrow you can have a day off. Chip will drive the truck and I'll clean the windows. You just come along for the ride."

"Great!" beamed Chuck.

Next day Chip drove the truck, and Chick did all the work. Chick was exhausted but Chuck was so happy he began to sing and dance in the back of the truck.